The Peace Dragon

Written by Linda Ragsdale

Illustrated by
Marco Furlotti

This is a story in which small explorations turn into giant adventures. It's about how the things we see aren't exactly what they seem... Sometimes they're better! (Or worse, but this is not that kind of story. Or at least not all of it is.)

This is the kind of story that starts on a perfect day for an expedition for an explorer named Sherwyn. Today he's happily wandered well away from home and stumbled over a sparkly stick. It seemed stuck.

So Sherwyn gave that stuck sparkly stick a GREAT BIG TUG...

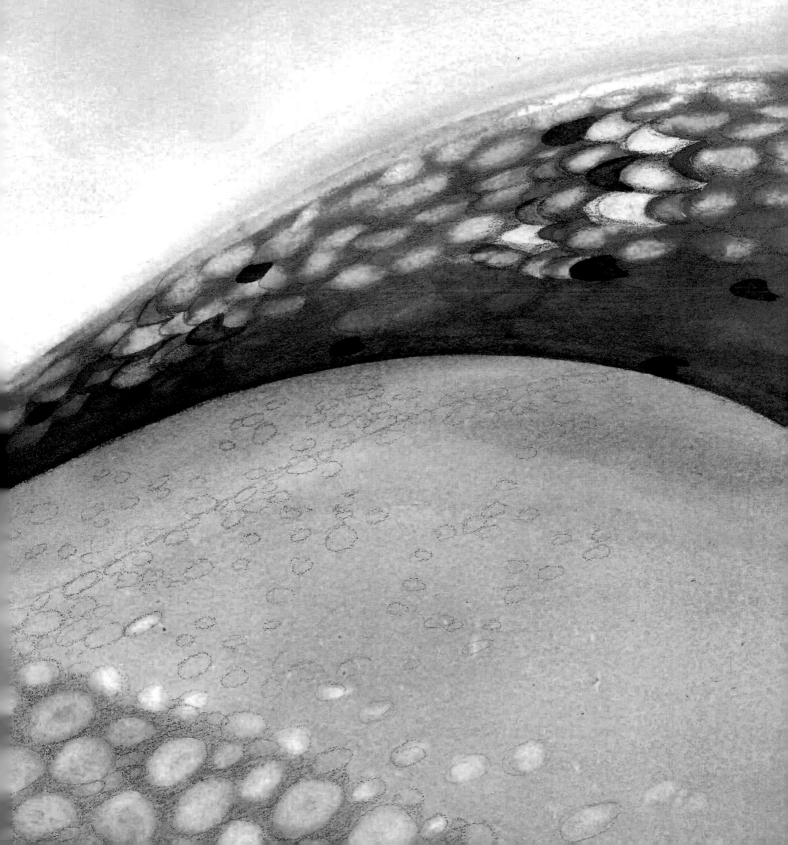

...and POP!
It wasn't stuck.
And it wasn't a stick.
It was a tail!
A tail belonging to a GREAT BIG DRAGON...

"Aaaaghhhhh!" cried Sherwyn.

The dragon just smiled.

GREAT BIG DRAGONS are not something you see every day. Someone else might have run away, but Sherwyn was curious, a bit confused, and maybe just a teeny bit afraid. After all, this was a dragon, but a smiling dragon.

"Why are you smiling?" he said.

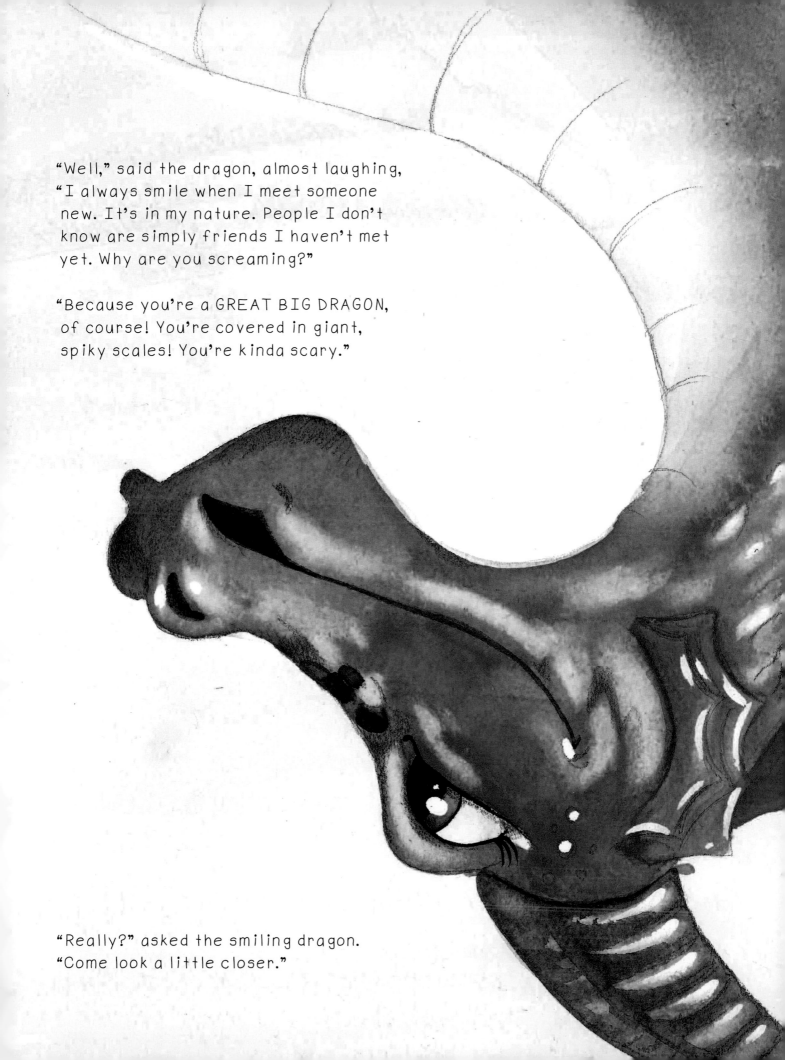

"Well," said the dragon, almost laughing,
"I always smile when I meet someone
new. It's in my nature. People I don't
know are simply friends I haven't met
yet. Why are you screaming?"

"Because you're a GREAT BIG DRAGON,
of course! You're covered in giant,
spiky scales! You're kinda scary."

"Really?" asked the smiling dragon.
"Come look a little closer."

Now, when a smiling dragon asks you to come closer, it may make good sense to pause. In some stories, getting close to a dragon can be a very bad decision. This isn't that kind of story. In some stories, an explorer may be too timid to get closer to a dragon. Sherwyn isn't that kind of explorer. Sherwyn stepped closer.

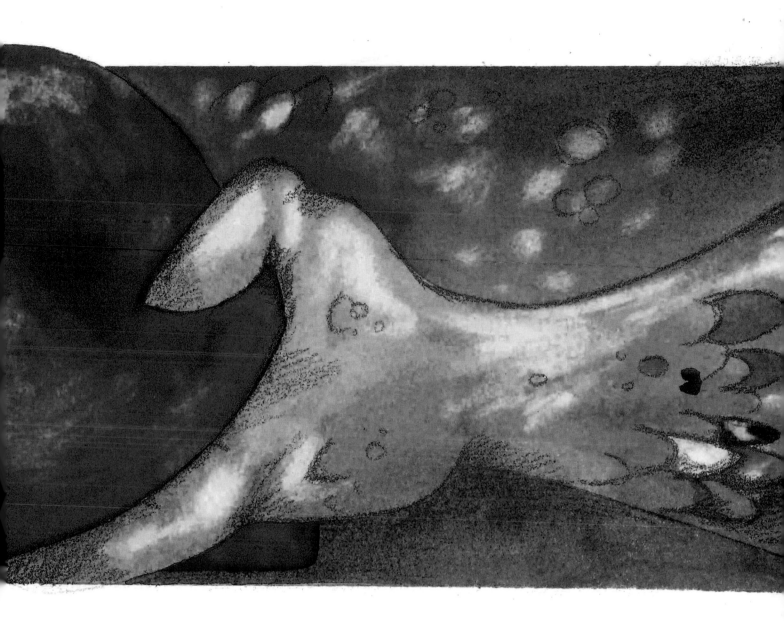

"My name is Omani and I am a Peace Dragon. I've devoted my
life to meeting and making friends and spreading a message of
peace and love. What you see as scary is actually the point of my
message," she said, slipping off a scale. "It starts with taking
time to see the whole picture. It is about greeting the world with
open eyes and an open..."

"HEART!" said a stunned Sherwyn. "You're covered in hearts!"

Sherwyn looked to see if he was covered with anything interesting. He was.

"I'm Sherwyn," he said. "I'm covered in...DIRT!"

They laughed and laughed, and the seeds of friendship were planted. From that day forward, Sherwyn and Omani set off on daily adventures, exploring every hill, field, and forest. The roots of their friendship grew deep.

One day, while resting in their favorite tree, Sherwyn finally asked Omani something that had been rolling around in his head for some time.

"You know, O, I've explored just about everywhere and I've never met a Peace Dragon. Where did you come from? Where do you live? Where've you been hiding?"

Omani laughed. "I haven't been hiding anywhere, Sherwyn. And right now I am from nowhere. I'm exploring. I've been wandering the world looking for a good place to live. You know, it is a little difficult for a dragon to find a loving home."

"WHAT?!? You have no home?" Sherwyn was stunned. "You've gotta come live in my village. You're gonna love my friends!"

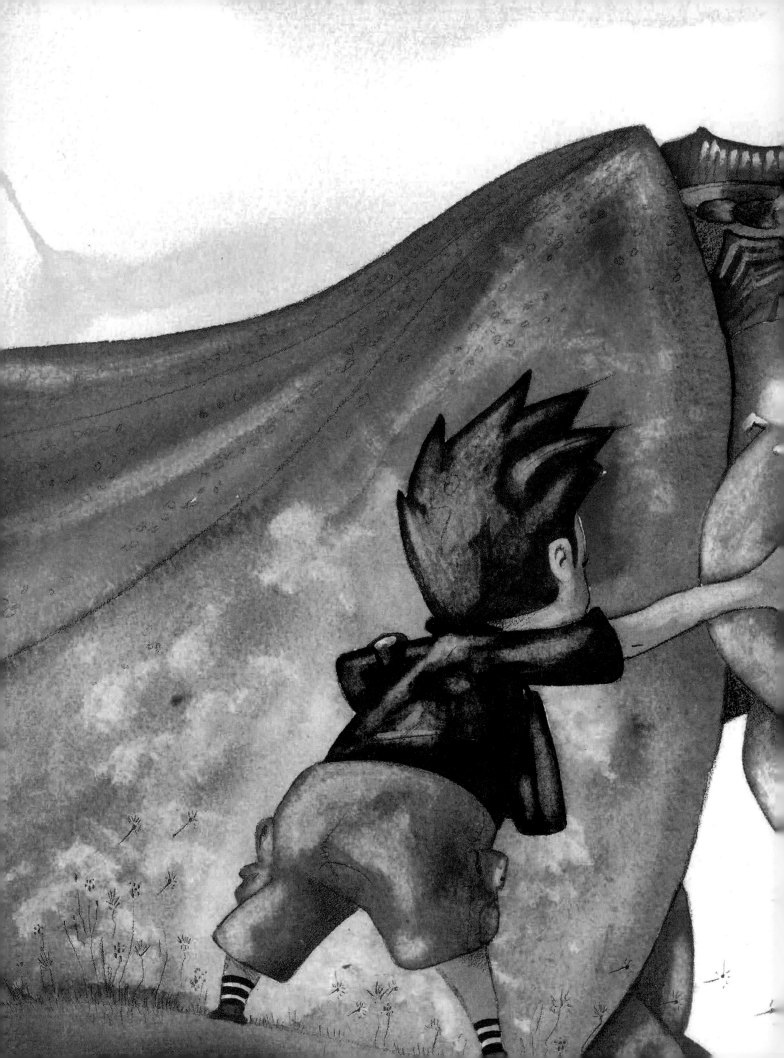

Omani smiled. "Thank you, Sherwyn. That's certainly bighearted of you, but I'm not sure this would work like you're thinking. The people in your village might not like it if you bring home a dragon. Dragons can be very scary. Remember, even you screamed when you first saw me."

Omani had a point, but Sherwyn was too excited to listen. All he could see was his friend.

"You're not scary at all! You're a Peace Dragon," Sherwyn said. "You're made of hearts and so are we. You'll see. Come on."

Sherwyn headed toward his village, assuming Omani would follow.

And follow she did. At first a bit skeptical, but then excited herself. "Maybe this time..." she hoped.

Because this is that kind of story.

Meanwhile, back in the village, everyone was going about their day as usual. A usual day consisted of people chatting in the streets, working together, lending a hand, and really just being nice to each other. They were people with kind hearts, just as Sherwyn had described them.

Sherwyn was so eager to introduce Omani to his friends that when he spotted the statue in the middle of town, he couldn't wait any longer.

"Race you to the statue!" he shouted.

Sherwyn dashed away.
Omani raced after him.

"STOP!"

cried Sherwyn.
"Please, stop."

Bumping and banging into itself,
the crowd stopped only inches
away from bashing into the two
frightened friends.

"This is my friend Omani," Sherwyn
explained. "She's a Peace Dragon."

"Dragons aren't peaceful!"

"Dragons are scary!"

"Dragons are nasty!"

Nobody was listening at all. Until...

"Wait! Look," said one gentle voice in the crowd, pointing at their shadow.
"Are we a nasty dragon?"

The whole crowd fell silent as they looked.
They were the only nasty dragon in sight.

Slowly the villagers began shuffling apart, and the shadowy shapes
became friendly, familiar faces.

Sherwyn showed them Omani's scales.
"She's made of all hearts."

Sherwyn told them why they were running.
"We were racing to meet you."

And very quickly that GREAT BIG DRAGON disappeared and Omani
the Peace Dragon appeared. The villagers' eyes were opened and
they could see what Sherwyn saw. They felt their hearts turn
toward love. Omani felt their love too.

She had finally found a loving home.

Sherwyn and Omani kept exploring, and wherever they went they shared Omani's message. The village embraced her message too. You might say Omani became the heart of the village.

In fact, Omani's message is also the heart of this story, and hopefully one day, it will be the heart of this world. Because while things can sometimes seem strange and scary, an open heart may reveal that they are friendly and loving. And if we choose, we can all live that kind of story.

"Greet the world with
open eyes and an open heart.
Use your heart as your compass
and keep your compass
pointed toward love."
–Omani

SEEING THE WHOLE PICTURE

Sometimes we don't take the time to look at the whole picture. Much like the townspeople when they saw Omani chasing Sherwyn, sometimes we can only see a small piece of the big picture. They believed Sherwyn was in danger by jumping to a conclusion. But as the townspeople learn, patience and an open heart play an important role in helping us see the whole picture. A puzzle is a great example of using patience and an open mind to see the bigger picture.

What you'll need:

• A puzzle (choose your puzzle size based on the age and number of people completing the activity)

What to do:
(Note: Before you begin, be sure your child does not see the final puzzle image until the very end of the activity!)
Ask your child to select a puzzle piece. Once your child has chosen a piece, ask them to guess what the puzzle depicts based solely on their individual piece. Once they have guessed, have them complete the puzzle. When the puzzle is complete, discuss how their guess differed from the final picture. Or if they were able to guess what the image is, discuss what led them to that conclusion. Finally, discuss how this applies to the townspeople from the story and the importance of seeing the whole picture.

A PEACE DRAGON'S PURPOSE

Omani's purpose is to spread peace and love to all those she meets. Her heart-shaped scales represent her purpose. However, Sherwyn didn't know that until he took a closer look. If you were to create your own dragon, what would your dragon's purpose be?

What you'll need:

• White copy paper
• Colored pencils, markers, or crayons
• A variety of art supplies

What to do:
Ask your child to draw a picture of a peace dragon and give their dragon a distinct quality that represents a chosen purpose. Their peace dragon can be a sports dragon that shares its love of playing games and is covered in soccer ball scales; a singing dragon that shares its beautiful voice with the world and always wears a music note hat; or any other peace dragon imaginable!

Once your child has completed their dragon, discuss what makes their dragon special and what about their dragon represents its purpose. Is their dragon's purpose visible in its appearance or would you need to learn more about their dragon to discover its purpose? Talk about how this relates to the first meeting between Sherwyn and Omani.

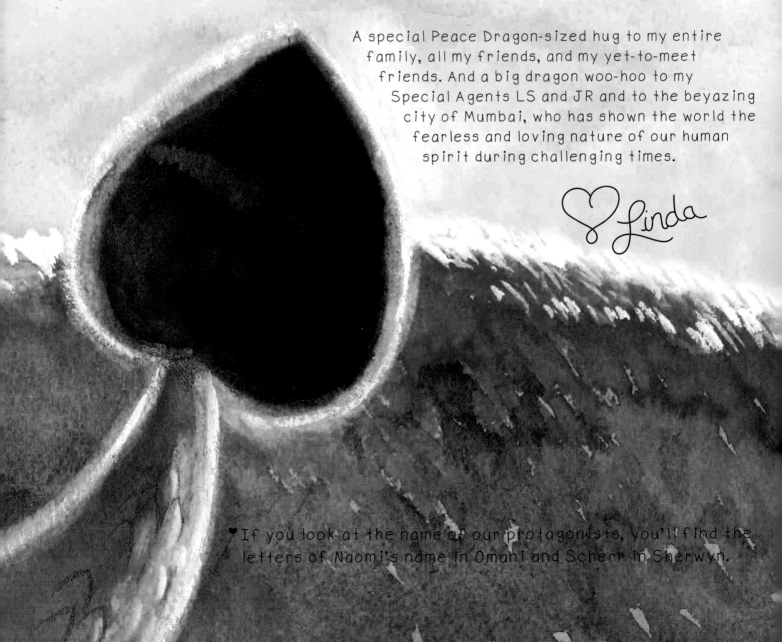

This story is dedicated to my friend Naomi and her father Alan Scherr. ♥

While traveling in Mumbai, India, thirteen-year-old Naomi Scherr and I were making our plans: break our somersault pool record; paint Mendhi designs on our feet; and I, being an illustrator, was honored when Naomi asked me to teach her how to draw dragons. I never had the opportunity to teach Naomi to draw her dragons, but I was inspired to start The Peace Dragon as a way to fulfill my promise.

As a Peace Dragon Ambassador, I travel the world teaching Omani's message. The children I meet learn to greet the world with open eyes and an open heart. They learn to use their heart as their compass and to keep that compass pointed toward love. One method I use for teaching is drawing a Peace Dragon with empty hands. To learn how to draw your own Peace Dragon (and discover why the hands are empty) please visit my website at www.ThePeaceDragon.com. I hope you're inspired to join Omani on her quest to bring peace into the world.

A special Peace Dragon-sized hug to my entire family, all my friends, and my yet-to-meet friends. And a big dragon woo-hoo to my Special Agents LS and JR and to the beyazing city of Mumbai, who has shown the world the fearless and loving nature of our human spirit during challenging times.

♡ Linda

♥ If you look at the name of our protagonists, you'll find the letters of Naomi's name in Omani and Scherr in Sherwyn.